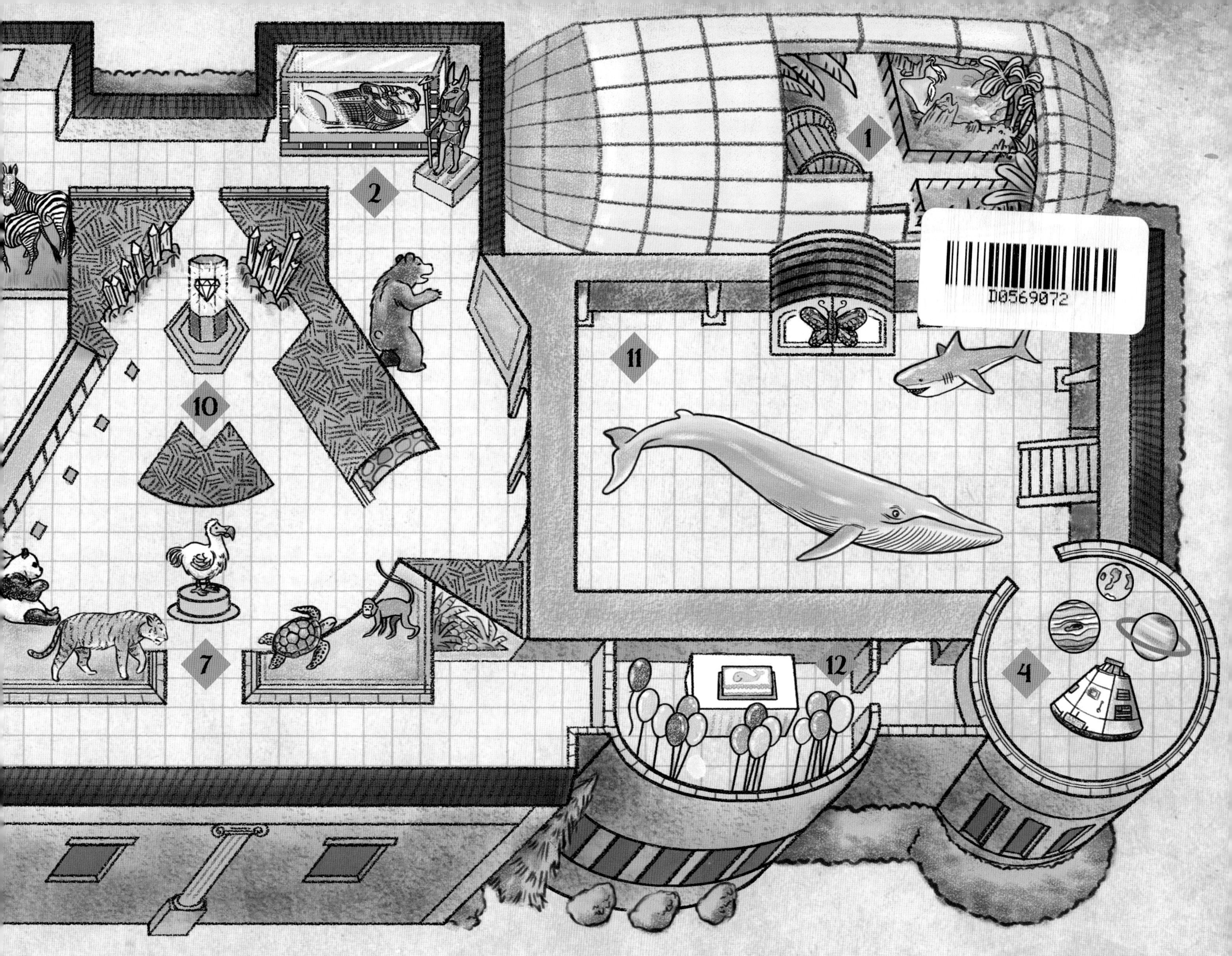

10. HALL OF MINERALS
11. HALL OF OCEAN LIFE
12. PARTY ROOM

MUSEUM OF NATURAL HISTORY

IMAX
THE PLANETS
DINOSAURS
MARINE MAMMALS
EXTINCT!

SLEEPOVER AT THE MUSEUM

Karen LeFrak
Illustrated by David Bucs

CROWN BOOKS
FOR YOUNG READERS
NEW YORK

Mason couldn't wait. Today was the best day of the year: his birthday! Tonight, he was going to have a sleepover party at the Museum of Natural History, his favorite place to visit.

Mason and his two best friends,
Zoe and Will, were ready for adventure.
Mason's parents led them inside.

They met their guide right next to giant fighting dinosaurs.

"Hi, guys. My name's Jesse," said a young man. "I'll be showing you around the museum. Follow me. I have a surprise."

"Welcome to the Discovery Room," said Jesse. "Tonight, you'll be going on a scavenger hunt. And if you solve all the clues, Mason can choose the hall for your sleepover."

Mason and his friends were excited. They loved solving mysteries.

"Here's how you wear a headlamp," said Jesse, demonstrating. "They're perfect for dark hallways."

He handed Mason the map and clue sheet. "If everyone's ready, let's get started!"

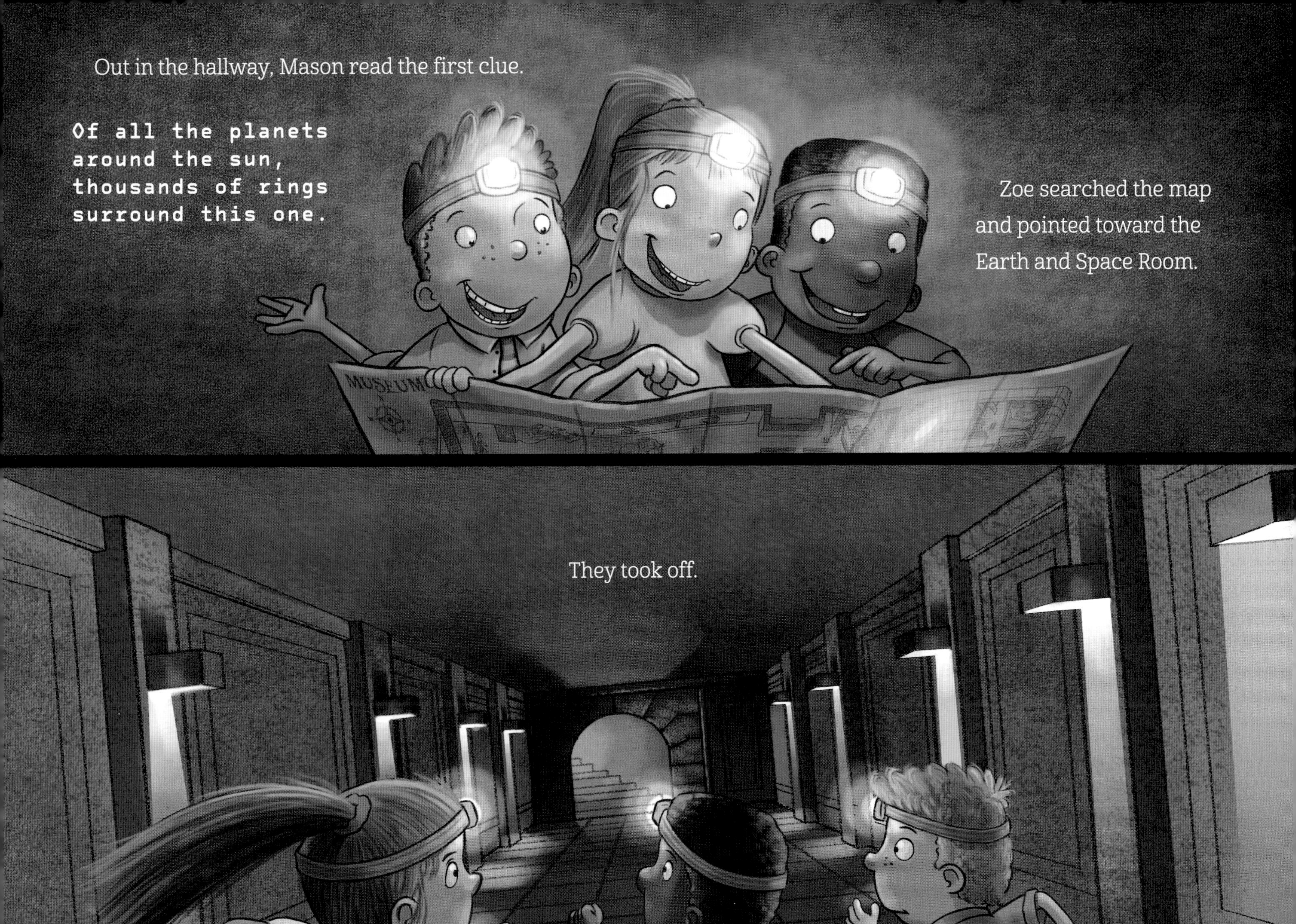

Out in the hallway, Mason read the first clue.

**Of all the planets
around the sun,
thousands of rings
surround this one.**

Zoe searched the map and pointed toward the Earth and Space Room.

They took off.

“There it is!” Zoe said. “The planet Saturn.”

Mason checked off the clue. First mystery solved.

They all laughed as Will pretended to be an astronaut taking giant, slow-motion steps on the moon.

But Saturn felt too far away from his own home planet. Mason would rather sleep somewhere else.

Mason's friends gathered around to hear him read the second clue:

He comes from an egg.
His size gives him fame.
This king of the reptiles
has quite a long name.

"Hey, I think I know this one," said Mason, smiling.

When they reached the Hall of Dinosaurs, the friends stopped in their tracks. *Tyrannosaurus rex* loomed over them.

"Look at this sign. It says he's the king of the dinosaurs," said Will.

"And dinosaurs were reptiles," added Zoe.

Mason checked off the second clue, while Zoe pretended she was a *Velociraptor*. Will studied the pterosaur flying overhead.

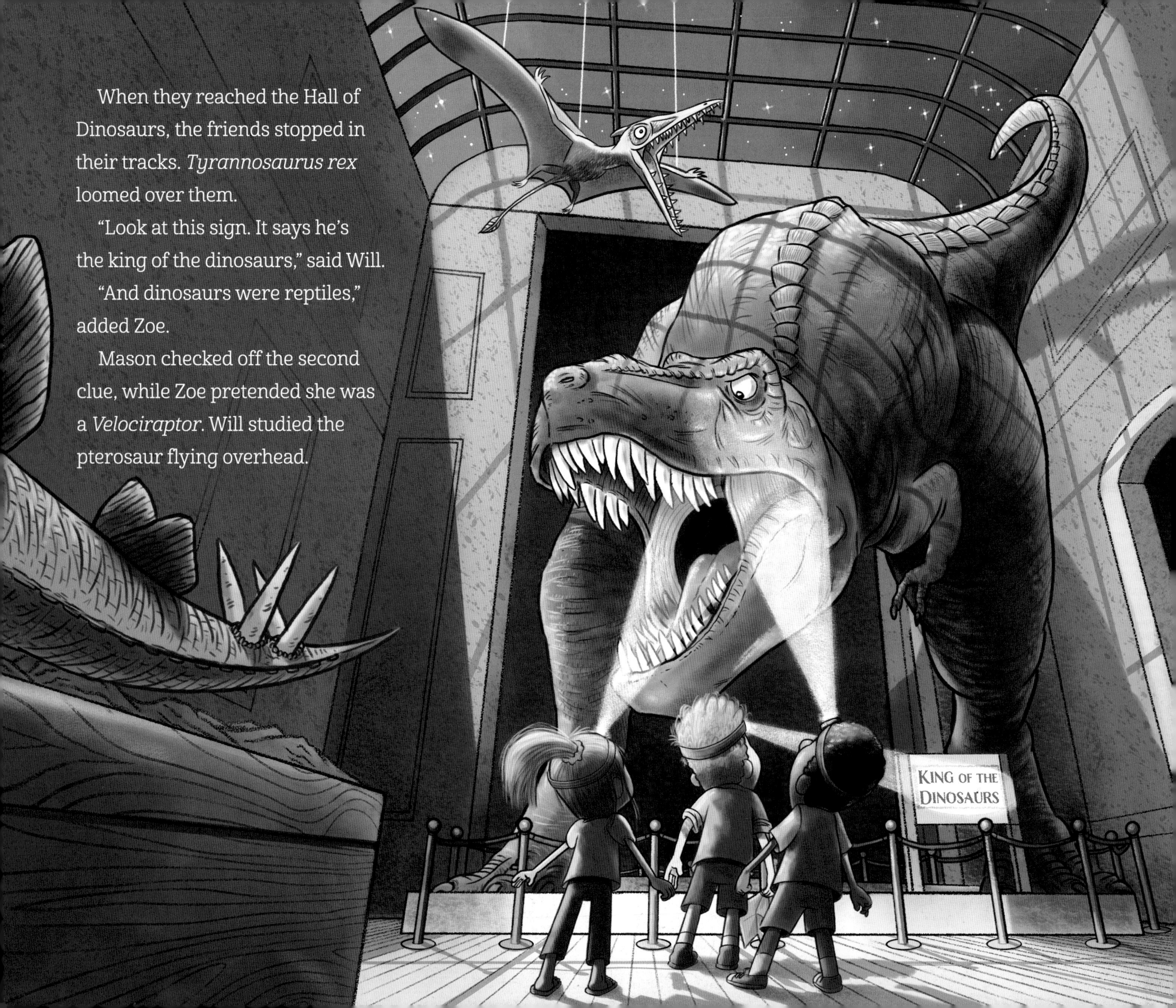

Mason thought his birthday was off to a great start. But he didn't think he could fall asleep with *T. rex* standing over them in the dark.

It was time for the third clue. Mason read:

`This mammal that uses his nose as a hose can wash his huge body and all twenty toes.`

"I've got this one," said Will, starting to run.

"We'll follow you," said Jesse.

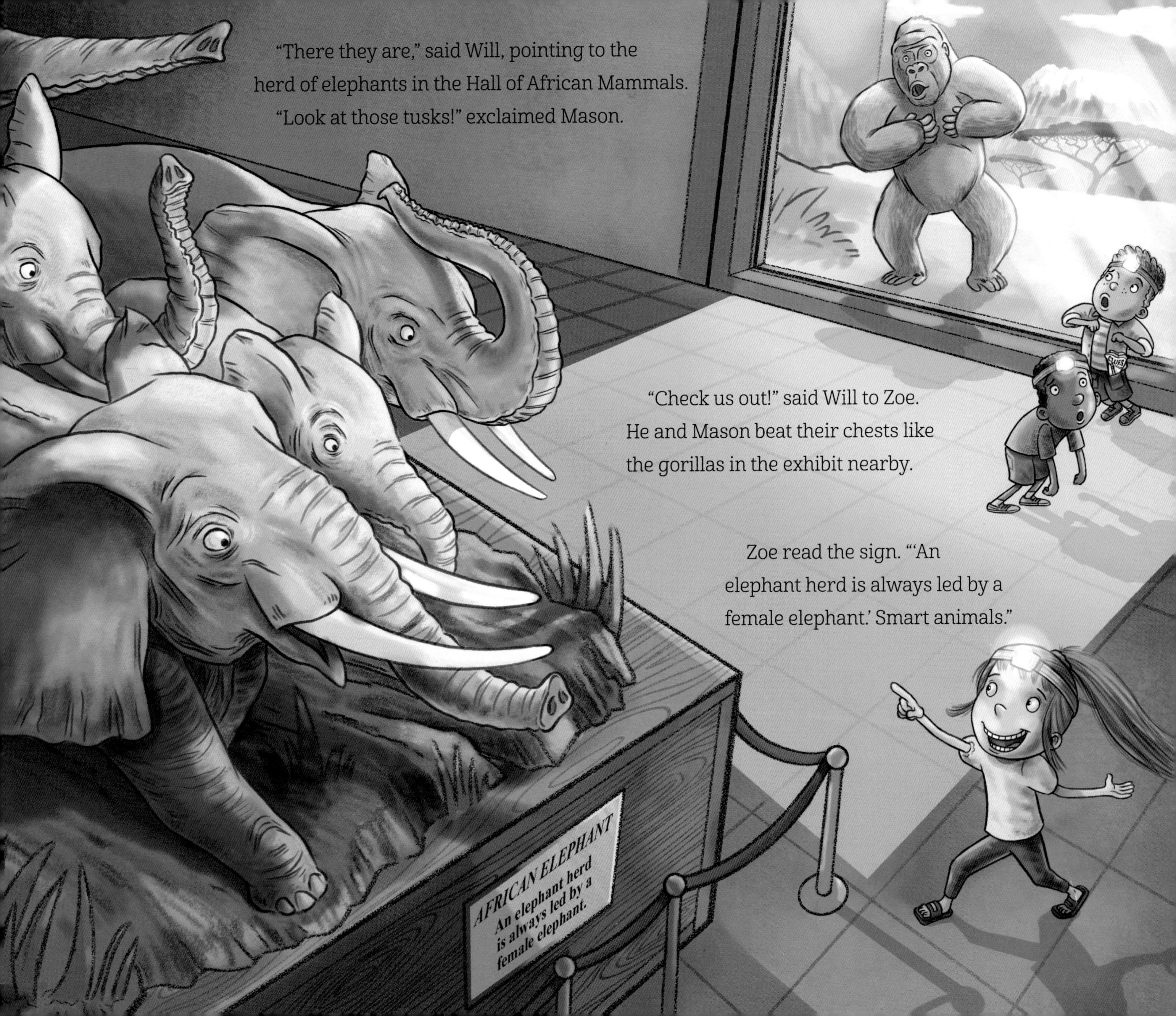

"There they are," said Will, pointing to the herd of elephants in the Hall of African Mammals.

"Look at those tusks!" exclaimed Mason.

"Check us out!" said Will to Zoe. He and Mason beat their chests like the gorillas in the exhibit nearby.

Zoe read the sign. "'An elephant herd is always led by a female elephant.' Smart animals."

Mason didn't think he could sleep while being stalked by a lion or stepped on by a giant elephant foot. What would be the best sleeping spot? he wondered.

"Can I read the clue this time?" asked Will. Mason nodded and handed him the clue sheet.

The hardest gems
you'll find on Earth
will dazzle you
for all they're worth.

"I'm stumped," said Will. Zoe pointed, and the boys followed.

“Just look at the diamonds sparkle!” Zoe said.

“You solved it!” said Mason. “It says right here that diamonds are the hardest minerals on Earth.”

The friends high-fived each other. They made a great team.

“Mining sounds like hard work,” said Mason, after reading a sign.

The Hall of Minerals was spectacular, but Mason didn't think he would sleep well here. Between glittering gems and thoughts of mining, he wouldn't be able to relax.

Mason read the next clue:

These birds had feathers
but could not soar.
They're now extinct.
There are no more.

"I know this one," said Mason. "It's this way."

They entered the Hall of Biodiversity, and Zoe spotted it first.

"The dodo bird!" she cried.

"Exactly," said Mason.

"You kids are amazing," said Jesse. "Let's walk through the Life on Earth exhibit. We can see 3.5 billion years of evolution in a few minutes."

Mason had learned a lot in the Hall of Biodiversity, but sleeping with the extinct predators would make him feel like prey.

"Two more clues to go, guys," said Mason.

```
These fragile insects—
queens or kings—
are always noticed
for their wings.
```

Will flapped his arms and said, "Follow me."

"Whoa!" exclaimed Will. "The Butterfly Pavilion feels like a rain forest."

"'Monarch' is another word for 'queen or king,'" read Mason.

"Right," said Zoe. "Then a monarch butterfly is a queen or king with wings!"

"Another clue solved," said Mason.

It was beautiful here, Mason thought, but the butterflies would probably tickle them while they slept. Plus, it felt as hot as a real rain forest.

Now he was getting worried—where *were* they going to sleep?

"It's our final clue," said Mason. "Let's read it together."

You've done so well.
It's getting late.
What can we eat
to celebrate?

"I know this one," said Will, rubbing his belly. "It's my favorite thing about birthdays."

"CAKE!" they yelled.

They ran all the way to the party room. When Jesse caught up, he congratulated them on solving every clue.

"We did it together," said Mason. "You guys are great friends and super at solving mysteries."

Jesse asked, "So have you decided where to sleep tonight, Mason?"

HAPPY BiRTHDAY, MASON

Mason took another look at his map. "I finally have the perfect place in mind. I'll take you there right after cake and presents."

"Another mystery," said Zoe.

"Soon to be solved," said Will, finishing his second piece of cake.

"This is it, the Hall of Ocean Life!" said Mason. "The best place to sleep in the museum. It feels just like being underwater."

He placed his sleeping bag directly below the blue whale, his very favorite animal.

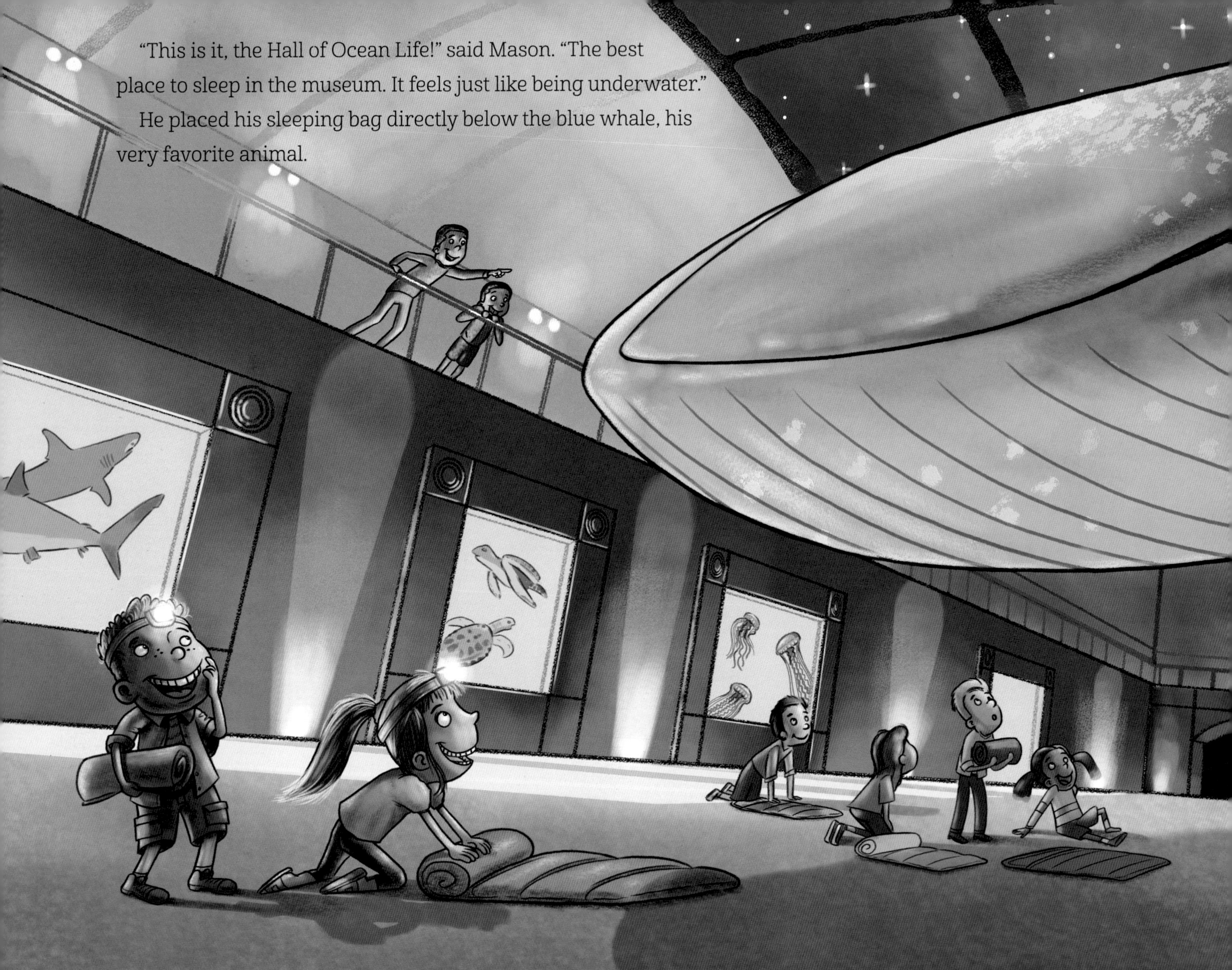

"Look," said Zoe. "The whale has a belly button, just like we do."

"You know what would be dangerous?" asked Will, looking at the open mouth of a great white. "Helping a shark brush its teeth."

Mason and Zoe laughed.

"We'd better brush our own teeth," said Zoe, yawning.

Sleepy at last, Mason imagined floating in the ocean, on top of the blue whale, and being gently rocked by waves. He gazed at the behemoth one last time before closing his eyes.

Then he whispered, "Good night, whale. Good night, friends," and fell fast asleep on his best birthday ever.

EXPLORE A MUSEUM NEAR YOU

Like Mason, Will, and Zoe, you can have fun and learn about the natural world by visiting a natural history museum. You can see artifacts and exhibits that relate to our past and present universe.

The Ashmolean, part of Oxford University, opened in 1683 and was the first natural history museum to grant admission to the public. It is not only Britain's oldest public museum, but possibly the oldest museum in the world.

Founded in 1812, the oldest natural history museum in the United States is the Academy of Natural Sciences in Philadelphia. Now part of Drexel University, it has a sleepover program called Night at the Museum.

There are many incredible museums all over the country—and all over the world—that you can visit. Some of the most notable that have sleepovers are:

1. **The Field Museum, Chicago**
   See Sue, the world's largest and best-preserved *Tyrannosaurus rex* fossil. **fieldmuseum.org**
2. **Perot Museum of Nature and Science, Dallas**
   Smell the beeswax of the Blackland Prairie or hear a prairie dog's alarm call in the Chihuahuan Desert. **perotmuseum.org**
3. **Natural History Museum of Los Angeles**
   Look a *Triceratops* in the eye! **nhm.org**
4. **Virginia Museum of Natural History, Martinsville**
   This museum has more than 10 million specimens in its collections. **vmnh.net**
5. **Arizona Museum of Natural History, Mesa**
   Uncover fossils in the Paleo dig pit. **arizonamuseumofnaturalhistory.org**
6. **American Museum of Natural History, New York City**
   Explore the 45 spectacular halls, and the Hayden Planetarium, at one of the largest natural history museums in the world. And if you share Mason's love of whales, don't miss the 94-foot-long model of a female blue whale in the Milstein Hall of Ocean Life. **amnh.org**
7. **Sam Noble Museum, Norman, Oklahoma**
   See the world's largest *Apatosaurus* skeleton. **samnoblemuseum.ou.edu**
8. **Carnegie Museum of Natural History, Pittsburgh**
   Find the two *Tyrannosaurus rex* skeletons posed in midfight. **carnegiemnh.org**
9. **Natural History Museum of Utah, Salt Lake City**
   Bring a bug to identify at the entomology center. **nhmu.utah.edu**
10. **Smithsonian National Museum of Natural History, Washington, D.C.**
    Let a butterfly sit on your shoulder as you stroll through the Butterfly Pavilion, or visit the world-famous Hope Diamond. **naturalhistory.si.edu**

Other places of interest, like zoos and aquariums, also have sleepovers for children and adults. Here are some of the most noteworthy:

Busch Gardens, Tampa
buschgardens.com

International Spy Museum, Washington, D.C.
spymuseum.org

Intrepid Sea, Air & Space Museum, New York City
www.intrepidmuseum.org

Milwaukee Public Museum
mpm.edu

Museum of Science and Industry, Chicago
msichicago.org

National Aquarium, Baltimore
aqua.org

National Baseball Hall of Fame and Museum, Cooperstown, New York
baseballhall.org

Philadelphia Zoo
philadelphiazoo.org

St. Louis Science Center
slsc.org

San Diego Zoo Safari Park
sdzsafaripark.org

Sea World San Diego
seaworld.com/san-diego

Zoo Atlanta
zooatlanta.org

How exciting would it be to experience a magical night at a museum for yourself!

ACKNOWLEDGMENTS

My appreciation goes to the dedicated and knowledgeable staff at the American Museum of Natural History in New York, especially Ellen Futter, Lisa Gugenheim, Jane Levenson, and Daniel Zeiger, for their guidance, fact-checking, and support during the creation of this book and for their commitment to sparking an excitement for learning in children and their families.

I am grateful to my editor, Emily Easton, for her guidance, expertise, and friendship.

For Ivan, Russ, and Polly —K.L.

For my museum buddies,
Yan and Lishu —D.B.

 Published in the United States by Crown Books for Young Readers, an imprint of Random House Children's Books, a division of Penguin Random House LLC, New York.

Crown and the colophon are registered trademarks of Penguin Random House LLC.

Visit us on the Web! rhcbooks.com

Educators and librarians, for a variety of teaching tools, visit us at RHTeachersLibrarians.com

Library of Congress Cataloging-in-Publication Data is available upon request.
ISBN 978-1-5247-7140-9 (trade) — ISBN 978-1-5247-7141-6 (lib. bdg.) — ISBN 978-1-5247-7142-3 (ebook)

MANUFACTURED IN CHINA
10 9 8 7 6 5 4 3 2 1
First Edition

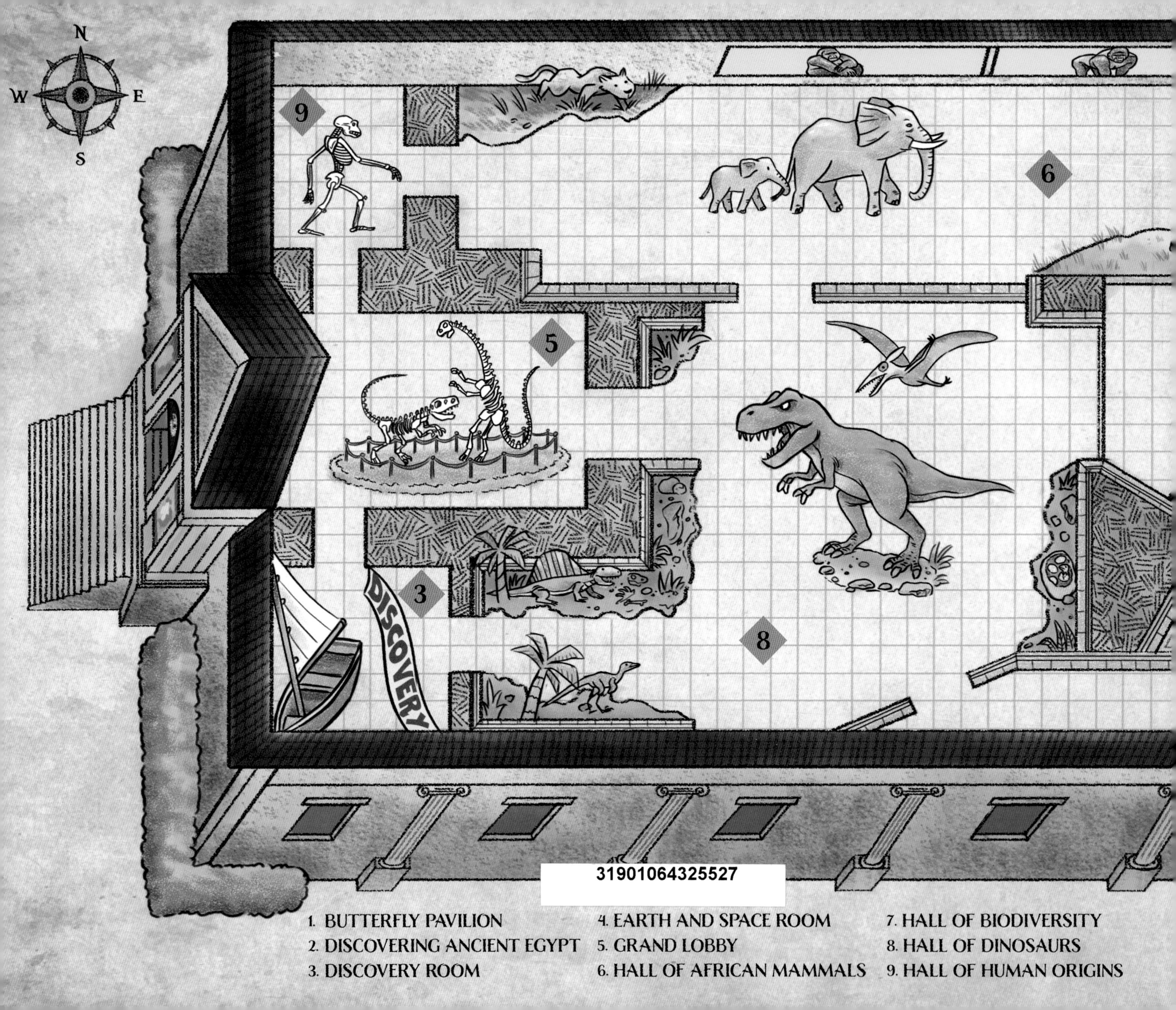
N
W
E
S
9
6
5
3
8
DISCOVERY
1. BUTTERFLY PAVILION
2. DISCOVERING ANCIENT EGYPT
3. DISCOVERY ROOM
4. EARTH AND SPACE ROOM
5. GRAND LOBBY
6. HALL OF AFRICAN MAMMALS
7. HALL OF BIODIVERSITY
8. HALL OF DINOSAURS
9. HALL OF HUMAN ORIGINS